This book is from the
Wyoming Elementary

P9-DHQ-532

Take a book ♥ Leave a book

This library is sponsored by
Wyoming United Methodist Church
5459 E Viking Blvd., Wyoming, MN 55092
651-462-5276 | wyomingunitedmethodist.org

Hampire!

Text copyright © 2011 by Sudipta Bardhan-Quallen

Illustrations copyright © 2011 by Howard Fine

All rights reserved. Manufactured in China.

No part of this book may be used or reproduced in any manner whatsoever without written permission

except in the case of brief quotations embodied in critical articles and reviews. For information address

HarperCollins Children's Books, a division of HarperCollins Publishers, 10 East 53rd Street, New York, NY 10022.

www.harpercollinschildrens.com

Library of Congress Cataloging-in-Publication Data

Bardhan-Quallen, Sudipta.

Hampire! / by Sudipta Bardhan-Quallen ; illustrated by Howard Fine. — 1st ed.

p.    cm.

Summary: Duck cannot sleep because he is hungry, but while he is preparing a snack, the Hampire, who roams the barnyard at night sinking his fangs into food, is creeping near.

ISBN 978-0-06-114239-0 (trade bdg.)

[1. Stories in rhyme.   2. Domestic animals—Fiction.   3. Vampires—Fiction.   4. Food habits—Fiction.   5. Humorous stories.]

I. Fine, Howard, date, ill.    II. Title.

PZ8.3.B237Ham    2011                                                                                     2009011750

[E]—dc22                                                                                                            CIP

                                                                                                                          AC

Typography by Jeanne L. Hogle

11  12  13  14 15   SCP   10 9 8 7 6 5 4 3 2 1

First Edition

To Penguino, my almost-vegetarian almost-barbarian
—S.B.Q.

For Little Mira
—H.F.

On the farm, the critters knew,
At night, while they were sleeping,
Past barn and pens,
Past lambs and hens,
A HAMPIRE went out creeping.

Some nights, they'd glimpse his red-stained fangs.

Each morning, they would find

Sprinkled on

The grassy lawn—

Red droplets left behind.

So while the moon shone in the sky,

They kept well out of sight.

When HAMPIRE roamed,

They all stayed home—

Until one fateful night.

A restless duck tossed in his bed.

"It's hopeless," he was mumbling.

"I've counted sheep

But cannot sleep

Because my tummy's rumbling!"

Poor Duck rolled left and then rolled right,

He sat up with a quack.

"It's risky, yes,

But I confess—

I need a midnight snack."

Just then, the HAMPIRE left his pen
In quite an awful mood.
His belly growled.
"I *need*," he howled,
"To sink my fangs in *food*!"

Duck scurried to the kitchen, where
He fixed a plate for nibbling.
Some jelly rolls,
And ice-cream bowls
With chocolate syrup dribbling.

Outside, the **HAMPIRE** sniffed the air.

His snout turned to and fro.

His fangs were bared,

His nostrils flared—

He'd sniffed out where to go.


So as Duck walked across the farm,

A shadow, grim and dire,

Crept near, tiptoe.

Duck screeched, "Oh no!

Here comes the fierce **HAMPIRE!**"

Duck stumbled to Red Chicken's coop
And roused Red from her slumber.
Inside, Duck cried,
"The HAMPIRE—hide!"
As outside, footsteps lumbered.

The HAMPIRE's fearsome face loomed near—
He'd climbed up on the stoop.
They took one look,
Red quaked, Duck shook,
Then both fowls flew the coop.

As Duck raced Red to Pony's stall,

They heard the **HAMPIRE** screaming.

"I'm starved, of course—

I'd eat a horse!"

His pointy fangs were gleaming.

Across the stable, Pony glimpsed

The **HAMPIRE**'s sniffing snout.

"What now?" asked Duck.

"We're out of luck—

It's time to chicken out!"

Pony gasped. "We've got to run!"
The birds climbed on her back.
Red sat stone-faced
As Pony raced
And Duck clung to his snacks.

"The HAMPIRE's on our tail!" Duck cried.
"Our goose is cooked indeed!"
The trio shrieked,
And when Duck peeked,
The swine was gaining speed.

"Which way?" asked Pony. "Over there!
I have a plan," said Red.
As HAMPIRE roared,
They headed toward
The old abandoned shed.

"Come here," the HAMPIRE bellowed, "please!
I'm hungry for a feast!"
But just before
He reached the door,
They slammed it on the beast.

The **HAMPIRE** pounded on the shed.

The wood began to shatter.

The floorboards creaked.

The hinges squeaked.

The shutters clanked and clattered.

"We're sitting ducks," poor Duck announced.

The shed had no back door.

Filled with dread,

He hid his head.

His snacks fell to the floor.

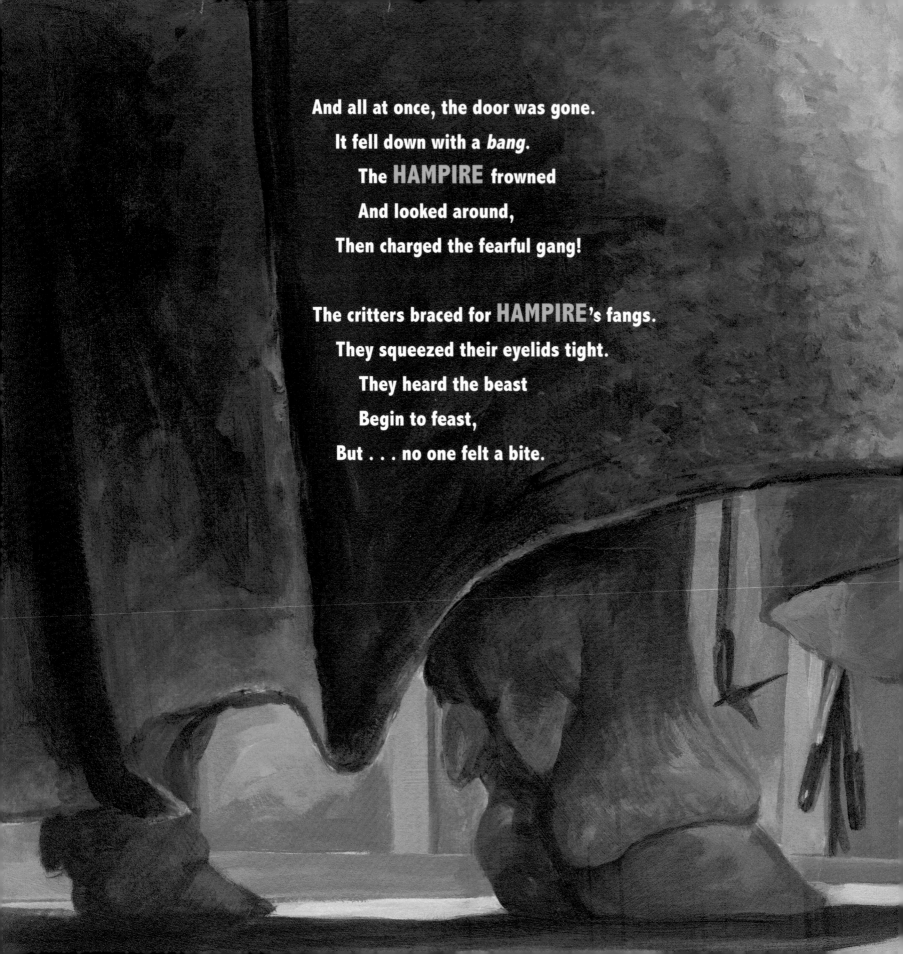

And all at once, the door was gone.

It fell down with a *bang*.

The HAMPIRE frowned

And looked around,

Then charged the fearful gang!

The critters braced for HAMPIRE's fangs.

They squeezed their eyelids tight.

They heard the beast

Begin to feast,

But . . . no one felt a bite.

Soon Duck peeked through his wings to see
How HAMPIRE filled his belly—
With bowls and bowls
Of jelly rolls,
His fangs all stained with jelly.

"He isn't eating us!" cried Duck.
"Of course! I'm no barbarian,"
Replied the swine,
"And when I dine,
I'm *always* vegetarian."

The critters stared in disbelief.
The duck was first to crack.
"A thrill, indeed!
But now I need
Another midnight snack."

They stormed the kitchen once again,
Then gathered 'round the fire.
As the host,
Duck made a toast,
"To our new friend, HAMPIRE!"